# ARE THERE STRIPES IN HEAVEN?

by
**LEE KLEIN**

*Illustrated by Pam Mauseth*

PAULIST PRESS

Library of Congress Cataloging-in-Publication Data

Klein, Lee, 1957-
    Are there stripes in Heaven?/by Lee Klein; illustrated by Pam Mauseth.
      p.  cm.
    Summary: Patrick's sister Colleen, a Down syndrome child, helps him to appreciate various experiences, including going to Mass and seeing their first rainbow.
    ISBN 0-8091-6618-6 (paper)
    [1. Christian life--Fiction. 2. Down syndrome--Fiction. 3. Mentally handicapped--Fiction. 4. Brothers and sisters--Fiction.] I. Mauseth, Pam, ill. II. Title.
PZ7.K678335ar    1994
[E]-dc 20

94-16351
CIP
AC

Published by Paulist Press
997 Macarthur Boulevard
Mahwah, New Jersey 07430

Printed and bound in the
United States of America

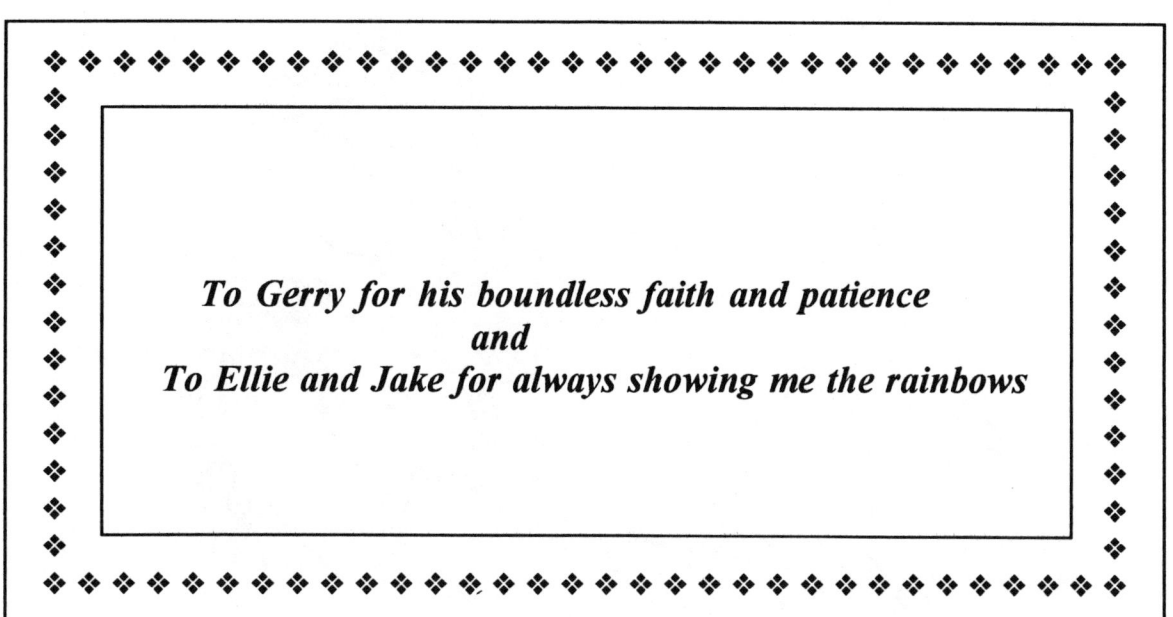

*To Gerry for his boundless faith and patience*
*and*
*To Ellie and Jake for always showing me the rainbows*

Special thanks to Mrs. Margaret Murphy's '93-94 fifth grade class at St. Anthony's School in Nanuet, New York.

My older sister Colleen is special. I don't mean
she's special just because she doesn't learn as fast
as other kids. Or because she doesn't run as fast or
climb as high as most people her age do. She's
special because she says things that other people
wouldn't bother to say. She's special because she
notices things that no one else bothers to see.
Yesterday Colleen did both of these.

It was Sunday morning. Colleen and I got dressed up for church as usual - almost.

"Patrick," she called from her room, "did you see a white ribbon? I need my ribbon for my ponytail."

"Oh, was that yours?" I asked, trying to sound innocent. The truth is, I needed string yesterday to tie up my lagoon creatures. They were captured by my army guys. Anyway, when I couldn't find any string...

"Sorry, Colleen," I said, untying the figures, "next time I'll ask you before taking your stuff."

"That's o.k.," my sister said, and she hugged me. "I love you, Patrick," she said, still squeezing.

"Fine," I said. "Then let go of me before you crush me."

The phone rang as we came downstairs to eat breakfast.

"Patrick, Doug is on the phone for you. Make it quick," Mom said.

"Mom, Doug wants me to go to Video World with him today! Can I go?"

"Sure, Pat. We'll drop you off at Doug's house on the way home from mass."

"No, Mom, he's leaving NOW. His parents said he could bring a friend and he wants to bring me."

"It's Sunday, Patrick. There are six other days during the week your friends can take you to Video World, but not this morning. The whole family is going to church together. Tell Doug you can go some other time."

"I never get to go anywhere special," I thought to myself.

In the car, I sat in the back seat with Colleen. I was still so angry that I wouldn't talk to anyone. My sister started singing, "If you're happy and you know it clap your hands," clap, clap...

"Patrick, why aren't you clapping?" she asked.

"Because I'm not happy. I'm mad!" I answered. It felt good to say something angry! Everyone was quiet for a minute; until Colleen started singing again, "If you're mad and you know it clap your hands," clap, clap. "Come on, Patrick, clap!" I didn't clap, but I smiled.

When we got to church, I held Colleen's hand as we crossed the parking lot. She was in a hurry to get inside. "Why are you rushing?" I asked. "It's the same thing every week."

"I like the same thing every week. I like to know what's going to happen next."

The congregation was singing the opening hymn. As we walked toward the front, we passed two girls I didn't know, but they looked about my sister's age. One of them had a long black braid. The other one had bracelets on both wrists.

They looked at Colleen, then looked at each other and giggled. "Look at that stupid ribbon in her hair," one whispered too loudly to her friend.

A few weeks ago we had sat down right in the same pew. When they saw us moving over in their direction, they shuffled out the other side. They wouldn't sit next to Colleen because she has Down syndrome. They treated her as though she had some disease they might catch, like chicken pox or whooping cough. They acted as though Colleen wasn't even a person.

Our priest, Father Jerry, was giving his homily on forgiveness. He said we should be as understanding and patient as Jesus tried to teach us. But I wasn't feeling too forgiving toward those girls. At the end of the Lord's Prayer, he asked us to shake hands and offer the "Peace of the Lord" to each other. Everyone shook hands and said "Peace" to anyone standing close by.

But Colleen rushed out of her seat. She began at the end of the first row and shook everyone's hand, looking straight into each person's eyes when she said "Peace." She went from row to row, stopping for each person. "Peace, Peace, Peace." She didn't miss a single one, not even an old woman who couldn't stand up. She even shook hands with a tiny baby.

Instead of facing the front, the whole congregation had now turned around backward to watch Colleen offering "peace" to the last few rows of people.

"Oh no!" said Dad. "She's disturbing everyone!"

"Patrick, go and tell Colleen to come back and sit down," Mom whispered.

"Oh, please, no, let her keep going," said a woman behind us. "She's so pleasant to everyone."

"Absolutely," agreed a man across the aisle. "Her enthusiasm is contagious!"

So I turned around too and watched my sister, just as she got to the last row. She stood in front of the same girls who had laughed at her.

"Peace," she chirped, looking straight into the face of the girl with the bracelets as she shook her hand. Before the other girl could get away, Colleen took her hand too.

"Peace," she repeated.

"Peace," replied the girl with the braid. The three girls held hands for a moment, then sat down together. This time, the girls didn't laugh at Colleen.

As soon as mass was over, Mom hurried through the crowd to find Colleen. Dad and I walked down the aisle toward the door.

"Dad, do you like going to church every week? Do you like it even though it's always the same?"

"I like coming to church very much, Pat. It's important to me, making time to pray with my family and friends. But, Pat, it's never the same every week. There's always something different to look for."

"Like what?" I asked.

"Look over there," he said pointing to the last row. There was Colleen, sitting on the pew. The girl with the bracelets was there too; she was braiding Colleen's ponytail.

"All set?" she asked, tying the white ribbon at the bottom of her braid.

Colleen nodded gratefully.

"O.K., see you next week."

Dad was right. That morning was different.

That afternoon it rained. It rained so hard we couldn't play outside. There wasn't anything good on television. I lay down on the couch, listening to the rain on the roof.

Colleen stood by the window with her face pressed up against the glass. "When can we go out?" she asked mother for the hundredth time.

"When the rain stops," repeated Mother.

I closed my eyes and thought about the fun I could be having at Video World. I thought about how there would be nothing special to do today, even when the rain stopped. Then I noticed the pattern of raindrops on the roof slowing down. A few seconds later, it stopped.

"When can we...?" started Colleen.

"NOW!" I answered and grabbed my baseball and mitt on the way out the door, not even waiting for my sister to catch up.

Colleen peered into a big puddle and looked at her reflection. I practiced catching pop flies.

"Look," she said.

"Yeah, yeah, I know, you can see yourself," I said, catching the baseball easily.

She took a pebble and threw it in the puddle, making a small splash.

"Look, Patrick, look!" she called.

"Yeah, I know, it makes rings in the water. So what?" I mumbled, wishing I had a friend who could hit the ball to me.

"Patrick, are there stripes in heaven?" Colleen asked quietly.

"What are you talking about now? Why would there be stripes in heaven?"

"Because I see them. Over there." She pointed over my shoulder.

Colleen did see stripes. It was a rainbow bending across the sky, over the houses behind us. I had never seen one before in real life. I could see it and through it at the same time.

"Wow," sighed Colleen.

"Yeah, too bad it will disappear soon."

"Good thing I saw it," she said quietly.

"It sure is. If it wasn't for you, I would have missed it."

I can go to Video World any day, I thought, but I might never see another rainbow again in my whole life.

We sat down together on the front step and watched the rainbow disappear.

"Colleen," I said, patting her on the shoulder, "if you're special and you know it, clap your hands." And she did.

FOR MORE INFORMATION ABOUT DOWN
    SYNDROME CONTACT:


NATIONAL DOWN SYNDROME SOCIETY
666 Broadway
New York, New York 10012

Phone: 1-800-221-4602



NATIONAL DOWN SYNDROME CONGRESS
1605 Chantilly Drive
Suite 250
Atlanta, Georgia 30324

Phone: 1-800-232-NDSC